COLORADO

I read it non-stop. I couldn't stop reading. It was (and is and will forever be) a beautiful piece of writing. My heart swelled…I was like a child, again, following the singsong poetic narrative. I fell in love with and for Maddie and Britney. I cried at the first punch. I was steeled knowing there had to be more…and there it was, served up; and I cried again. It will turn our world upside down AND it will make us ask questions, lots of questions. The reading experience was like being in a lyrical version of Carl Sagan's Contact, but with a twist. Through its whimsy and charm, it astonishingly answers the existential question: "Who are we and why are we here?" No doubt the author, a strong man of faith, will be branded a heretic for dare opening a steel door that few wanted pulled back to reveal that the Mysterim Tremendum was love, forgiveness and mercy.

CARL BRACKPOOL
CEO of an International Technology Company

PENNSYLVANIA

I say this with absolute conviction: the world needs comfort and kindness – warmth and goodness. *The Address of Happiness* will awaken you, stir you, enlighten you, inspire you, ignite you and empower you to fill this world with beauty. The world needs this book now more than ever. May it do for you what it did for me – fill you to the brim with hope and aspiration to find the kingdom of love within!

AMY FERRIS
Author, Marrying George Clooney

ILLINOIS

I feel that I have just read a parable...a story to tell a truth. I am over-whelmed with emotion. I find in Happiness a message that is very similar to what I found in John Wesley, a love that is always within, seeking to find expression and response, the gospel message in more modern terms. This story is the message of life - always moving forward into the limitless unknown, always seeking the best, the more perfect. Happiness resolves the mystery of human relationships by celebrating the love between the two persons involved. I loved the message.

REV. DR. DONALD BLACK
United Methodist Minister

TEXAS

"She could not wait to be born and begin her search for the one her heart loved." So begins the remarkable journey of Maddie and Britney, two gentle souls matched in Heaven and destined to meet on the earthly plane (and even beyond). Their quest to hear each other's inner celestial "music" animates this lovely, poetic fable, which has much to teach about the divine melody of Love that resounds within us all. During their search for each other, I was reminded of Audrey Hepburn's wonderful line in the classic film *Sabrina*, when her father chastises her for dreaming too much, for "reaching for the moon." No, Audrey says, "The moon is reaching for me." Mr. Kirkpatrick's luminous new book is spellbinding. I couldn't put it down.

REX MCGEE
Writer, Teacher, Father

CALIFORNIA

I remember feeling enlightened after reading Jonathan Livingston Seagull. *The Address of Happiness* gave me a similar – even more spiritual – sense of tranquility. *The Address of Happiness* is a gift to the Universe – and perfectly timed. It beautifully captures the fact that love transcends all else. When I put the book down, I felt as if I'd been for a swim in a lake of serenity. It is a remarkable journey that reconnects us with the sacred.

DOUG COLLINS
Director for a Not For Profit

IDAHO

As a secular humanist with spiritual longings - one who believes, like Emerson, in a direct relation to God (read: the great mysterious universal presence), I found *The Address Of Happiness* an irresistible invitation to a loving, and gentle relationship to what the poets call, Mysterium Tremendum. If all of us could have the enormous faith that the remarkable Maddie and Britney have in this wonderful journey – what a world it would be! If nothing is impossible for love, how can we ever be against it?

SAMANTHA SILVA
Author, Once Upon a Carol

FLORIDA

Music has no need for language in its quest to connect the disconnected. It is apt that *The Address Of Happiness* uses music as the connective tissue of its story of transcendent love and beauty. Like a beautiful melody it is said that the simple act of smiling can be a transformative experience. Sit back, focus your attention and get ready. *The Address Of Happiness* will prepare you for a life of smiles and provide you with the tools to change your world and the world around you.

CHRIS BOARDMAN
Professor – Frost School of Music, University of Miami

NEW JERSEY

The Address of Happiness is a gorgeous work of whimsical fiction. Not only does this book lift you up, it cradles you in its warm embrace and holds you for that extra squeeze. It is a modern meditation on fate, acceptance and, above all, love...a gentle reminder which, frankly, I needed in my life at the moment more than I ever realized.

PAUL RUSSELL SMITH
Writer, husband and father of three

MARYLAND

If, indeed, we do believe that each of us is created in God's own image, that each and everyone one of us is a lily in His field, then we are going to need more stories like *The Address Of Happiness* which so lyrically illustrates this point. Could this be *Love Story* for the new millennial reader? Let us hope.

MARYKAY POWELL
Motion Picture Producer, Random Hearts

WISCONSIN

Love is the universe's greatest mystery and greatest truth. Among two members of the same species, who among us dare to defame God's blessing of it?

JOEL ROGERS
Professor of Law, Political Science, Public Affairs and Sociology – University of Wisconsin

MASSACHUSETTS

The Address of Happiness is beautiful and thought provoking. I found myself rereading many passages to absorb the meaning. It inspires a desire for a deeper conversation on levels of love, life, religion, spirituality and humanity. I have struggled with trying to find my place as a gay person and gay parent for years. So much of this story resonates. I felt it described the root of the inner turmoil of Maddie quite well. As someone who in this part of my life identifies as an atheist with an open mind, *Happiness* made a seamless connection between the spirit of creation and love. I felt this was quite powerful and left me exploring my own beliefs.

MONICA BAUTISTA
Single Working Mom of Two

SOUTH CAROLINA

This is a love story that rips through the boundaries of our earth-bound imagination and takes us to the divine! *The Address Of Happiness* will make you believe, once and for all, that everlasting love is truly possible. The beautifully written prose allows the reader to fall hopelessly in love with Love. Every page of this book is a gift! A thought-provoking, mesmerizing delight! I cannot wait to read it again.

DEBORA BAKER
Artist

NEW YORK

I'm a rabbi, so I support marriage equality. My support of marriage equality is an expression of my faith. It arises from fundamental principles found in the Hebrew Bible and the rabbinic tradition, among them, that each human being is made in the divine image, that affording full dignity to every person is a religious obligation, and that we are commanded to pursue social justice. It arises from the biblical injunction that it is "not good" for a person to be alone, and that the opportunity to create a family is an essential aspect of our humanity, and of our obligation to express, as fully as possible, the image of God reflected within.

RABBI JAN UHRBACH
Conservative Synagogue, Sag Harbor

GEORGIA

I understand what it means to be completed in another. I lost the one I was meant to love. *The Address of Happiness* encourages me to hope for a day when my love will be restored.

WINDSOR RUCH
Marketing Executive

* These addresses represent a sampling of a worldwide response to *The Address of Happiness*. For more, visit theaddressofhappiness.com

"Addresses from the World"

ENGLAND

I am far from America, but I am right at home, having just read *The Address Of Happiness*. What a beautiful and touching story! When I read of the author's aunt who inspired the story, I could only think that she must be very proud. There is no doubt that she is smiling from Heaven, believing in the power of God who pushes mankind forward to a shining destiny.

ILEEN MAISEL
Producer, The Golden Compass, Romeo and Juliet

CHINA

There are no boundaries if we believe in the power of love. *The Address of Happiness* is a beautiful gift to all of us who dream of a better world.

MARS LU
Doctor of Medicine

BRAZIL

The Address of Happiness impresses with its wit, intellect and compassion. This piece of prose poetry is an uplifting reminder of how love conquers all. Two people, regardless of who they are, meant for each other, can make this world a better place. It is a poignant and powerful read, sometimes whimsical, often more than a little sad, a metaphor for life. I thoroughly enjoyed it and will continue to reap the benefits of its message, as I hope other's will.

BILL DIX
Project Manager

AFRICA

The delight in reading *The Address of Happiness* is that it presents the complexity of life in a way that is enlightening and uplifting. The clear, almost musical prose tells a story of life and love through one of the burning issues of our time - same sex marriage - putting love into a perspective that all can appreciate and understand. I found myself reading passages from the book aloud, because the cadences of the sentences were a bit like a children's book with the solemn, reassuring quality of a church service. *The Address of Happiness* has a universal appeal that will find readers in all parts of the world because of its clarity and joy.

ANDREW MELDRUM
Associated Press, Johannesburg

ARGENTINA

The Address of Happiness is just what you need when "they" make you feel it is a sin every time your heart beats. I hope this comforting and magical story will help everyone understand the music of God's heart. I loved it!

MARCOS DUSZCAK
Documentary Filmmaker, Familias Por Igual

CANADA

The Address of Happiness is a simple tale with a profound impact. Laurens van der Post once wrote: "The story is like the wind. It comes from a far off place and we feel it". This is how I felt about David Paul Kirkpatrick's, *The Address of Happiness*. Kirkpatrick shines a great and insightful light on love. What a wonderful reminder of the transcending power of love and a true gift for all those who read it!

LISA TOWERS
Executive Producer, The Christmas Choir

The ~Address~
of Happiness

A Love Story

David Paul Kirkpatrick

HAPPINESS

The Aaddress of Happiness
Copyright 2012 by Happiness Publishing with Heart Publishing, All rights reserved
    Imprint of FirstWonder LLC
Cover Design by Chris D'Antonio

Kirkpatrick, David Paul
        The Address of Happiness / David Paul Kirkpatrick
                p. cm.
        ISBN-10: 0972644717 (hardcover)
        ISBN-13: 978-0-9726447-1-6 (hardcover)
        1. Allegory   2. Fiction   I. Title
        TXu001813616 / 2012-06-04

Printed in United States of America

13 13
1   2

Foreword

by Stephen Simon

Every great love story has at least one element in common—the obstacles that the lovers must overcome.

In literature and movies, from *Romeo and Juliet* to *Gone With The Wind*, from *West Side Story* to *The Way We Were*, the deeper and more formidable the challenges to love, the more their resolution resonates in our hearts and souls.

In my life, I was blessed to be involved with a love story, the film *Somewhere in Time* which I produced in 1979, in which the prime obstacle was time itself.

With *Somewhere in Time*, we also faced the obstacle of a film world that was much more interested in dance, action, and light fun in 1980 than in a gentle movie about two people who literally will themselves to meet, even though they faced the slight logistical challenge of one of them having to journey several decades back in time to meet the other. Fortunately, Christopher

Reeve chose *Somewhere in Time* as his first film after *Superman*. (Years later, after Chris' tragic accident, I think that film's Superman became a real life superhero whose courage would inspire millions of people....then and forever.)

The Address of Happiness has the great good fortune, I believe, to be published at just the right time. In fact, the most exquisite of times. To paraphrase an old saying...when the world is ready, the story—and the storyteller—arrive.

As far as obstacles in a story itself are concerned, *Somewhere in Time* was kindergarten and *The Address of Happiness* is grad school.

Two kindred souls connected in and by spirit are born in separate countries and then, even though they have lost any conscious memory of each other, somehow must find a way to reconnect....in a world populated by billions of people. *The Heart is a Lonely Hunter* indeed.

When David Kirkpatrick, whom I've known and deeply respected for over twenty-five years, asked me to read this book, I had no idea what a transformative experience the journey would be. I opened the book, started reading, and time folded in on itself.

I didn't stop reading for a single moment and, all of a sudden, I had finished.

In truth, I have no memory of even breathing during that time and I'm still more than a bit bedazzled by what awaits you in these pages.

We so often forget how beautiful we humans can be as a species when we operate at our very best. *The Address of Happiness* reminds us of that beauty and is also a loving and gentle reminder of our exquisite capacity to both love and forgive.

This book has helped me feel good again about simply being human, and I hope the extraordinary journey of the lovers in these pages will echo that way in your own heart as well.

Or, come to think of it, maybe the moment has now arrived in which we will see the love story you are about to encounter as being in fact an ordinary, every day journey experienced by millions of people everywhere on this beautiful planet.

And then, Dorothy, we will know that we are somewhere over the rainbow at last.

Stephen Simon
West Linn, Oregon

"We were together.
I forget the rest."

- Walt Whitman

In a twinkling land far from time, there is a place where the Music always rises.

There, Love is full of surprises.

Like smoke from a chimney, like mist on a warming lake, the Music lifts revealing gifts.

All carry thorn, all shall adorn.

Here, Britney and Madeline met before they were born.

I mention, without exception.

All are loved.

What did you say?

All are loved.

What do you say?

I say, run and play!

Play?

Yes, you will find me at the start.

But where?

In your heart.

My heart?

What is a heart?

And you will find me in those you love.

Who are they?

They are my lovelies.

And you?

I am Love.

And no more asking was necessary.

For the beginning was and is and forever Love.

And in this starry place so distant, the Music rose.

All were floating without clothes.

There was no shame; no one to blame.

This land, no mind like ours could know!

Light as snow.

Small as a pea.

Wider than the sea.

This is where you and I came to be.

There was the gentle sound of rain.

The sweet echo of stars breaking and converging.

Where Love was merging

There was the song of sparrows, and the chirping of the larks.

In the distance, the sounds of happy children in the parks.

When Love blinked, the heavens sang.

Everywhere the bells rang.

And in the Music, souls began to talk.

And hearts reached to walk.

Oh, I love you!

How can this be?

I was made for you!

You will find me, won't you?

But how?

You'll know me by my eyes.

What are eyes?

And in this sacred place, many made plans
to sing their songs.

Some would sing alone.

Some would form a quartet.

Yeah, man, don't forget…

…Me!

Others would make an orchestra.

They were a few who'd start a rock n' roll band.

One would name his new home "Graceland".

All would make a family.

But what is a family, anyways?

Well, there is Love.

And while Love dreamed,

Britney and Madeline met in this place before

yesterday and after tomorrow.

For the harsh hands of Time were not there to greet you.

So wonderful to meet you!

Your eyes have such a touch.

Do you think we might sit and just stare at one another?

Oh, I would like that very much!

What is sitting?

Flying without moving.

So they flew steady.

Never ready.

To move on.

For a blink of an eye.

Or a year or two.

They were stuck like glue.

Everything seemed forever new.

What are those glorious dots?

Those, dear one, are forget-me-nots!

In their eyes, they saw the kindness in the other. There was no need for another.

For there was just no other way.

And like all the musicians,

They, too, planned.

They would be a duet.

They would be happy.

What is happy, anyways?

To answer, Britney turned Madeline's face toward the horizon.

It's walking together in the same direction.

There, just beyond the edge was the Mysterium Tremendum.

Within, lay the golden story filled with the glory of each of us.

No box, nor sea, nor me would be compromising the sweet surprising of that Music rising!

Like a feather sweeping through weather,

The arrows flew.

Oh! There goes me!

Oh! There goes you!

Time did fly.

But why?

What is Time doing here?

Was this not what poets call "Paradise"?

What's a poet?

This was and is the age of twinkling goodbyes with the wonder of opening eyes.

Where we start the race of finding heart.

To the land of Nod set apart,

from this radiant mystery of Love!

What shall we recall?

If anything at all?

Find yourself in my eyes, you were there from the start!

Will you carry me in your heart?

Of course, we were meant to be together!

And how could they not?

For they were from Love.

They were meant for meaning.

As I go along, do me no wrong.

Love me!

If anything breaks down, I'll be around.

Find me!

So Love knit Madeline into her mother's womb.

The loom spun. The work was done.

Find Me!

And Love was overcome.

For it was as if Madeline was the first and only one.

Now, isn't that just like Love?

Elaine and Ben Eaves had really wanted a child. They would name her "Madeline" if she was a girl, or "Tom" for a boy. They had tried for years without conceiving, there was some vague talk of Elaine leaving. She was a tiny woman with aquiline features. Ben was a bear of a man. They seemed incongruous, the bird and the beast, but Love had brought them together.

Ben played rugby at Saint Patrick's University in London, Nod. Elaine fell in love with him from the stands.

Still, years flew by. They turned to the latest in science to help them.

They put their faith in the laboratory and their

hopes into a test tube.

For they were a thoroughly modern couple.

He was so tall. She was so small! Sometimes, they thought there would be no baby at all.

Ben proclaimed the power of science and the achievements of men. He was an engineer and was hopeful about the future cities that men would build.

Sadly, he forgot about the twinkle in Love's eyes.

In the midst of the labs, the clinics and anguished trial, Elaine became pregnant after awhile.

Ben drove his Volvo to the glass house they called home.

"I can't believe that it's happened!" Ben said, taking Elaine happily into his arms.

"Our baby is a miracle!" cried Elaine.

"Of science!" Ben proclaimed.

Little Maddie poked and prodded her mother all through the pregnancy.

The truth is, Maddie didn't want to be born at all.

She wanted to stay with Britney in the celestial sphere, and linger forever without coming here.

"Oh my!" Elaine sighed. "Honey, feel the kick."

And Ben put his hand upon her stomach.

Krr- puuut!

"She will be quite a dancer!" Ben laughed.

Elaine was in her ninth month and second week.

Maddie thought there was no reason for this race in some unknown place.

In a land where she was getting a face!

Whhhhahhhhhh!

Finally, the doctors at London Hospital decided they needed to perform a caesarean.

And so, out of life's longing for itself, it began.

So Maddie swam.

Come back for just a little while, Britney cried.

Before Maddie could answer, she was swept beyond the numerous stars.

And there was no way she was going back through Mars!

But, Maddie knew she would find Britney, yes, she would find her without rest.

On a rainy day in London, Maddie was born into consciousness.

Madeline Lauren Eaves was twenty days late. *(As was her fate, she would be perpetually late with most everything in her life.)*

She came into life bawling and kicking.

Maddie weighed eight pounds two ounces with eyes wide open as she was looking for something.

She was a happy child, ever curious, ever watchful, always looking for Britney.

Maddie lay in the grass and watched the lady-bugs. She turned on her back and saw the stars.

Yes, there was that lovely land beyond Mars!

Her capacity to love and care poured out of her.

She loved the city playground, not so much for the carousels and the slides, but because of the boys and girls.

She kept them from knee scrapes, tumbles and fumbles. She waited at the bottom of slides to catch the jumbles.

As a five-year-old, she made castles in the sand recalling Music land.

Later, as she grew, her eyes drifted away from castles and cloud. She heard London calling, very loud.

Like her father experienced before, Maddie no longer saw the door to heaven's shore. There was no twinkle. No periwinkle.

Yet, the song was there in her heart. It would always be there. It was there from the very start.

Often Maddie would go to the window at night. She would watch the fair stars shine.

For her seventh birthday, her mother bought her a telescope.

"To our daughter – the girl that science has made!" Ben said, puffing his machine-man chest as he stood over the birthday cake.

Maddie loved staring out at space, and Elaine thought the telescope might encourage her daughter's worldly pursuits.

Elaine would feel a tug at her heart when she would look into Maddie's room at night. There she saw her daughter peering through the telescope at the vast universe before her.

Her daughter's own sad search was Elaine's as well.

"What does it all mean?" Maddie would say to herself.

In the stars that seemed to shiver in the blue darkness, she looked for the answers.

She heard the Music call her name.

But in the glass house that science built, she could not hear the Music of her heart.

There were no paintings on the walls. Her father had called her a dancer, even though there was no dancing in the glass house. Others might be in a rock 'n roll band. Some might live in Graceland. But no, not Maddie.

She was a stranger in the land of Nod.

Oh, yes, for sure she was awed.

How could you not be?

Her love was in the sky as it is for all lovers, including you and I.

It is that great stir in a star that beckons us to discover who we really are.

For what is a poet without such a dream?

But Maddie was a child of science. She was seven years old and she could no longer find the Music.

Sadness lengthens the hours.

How we spend our days is, of course, how we spend our lives.

In a small town in American town on Nod, Hazel Hoppenfop was panicked.

She was sixteen years old and pregnant.

Hazel had never had a boyfriend. She was plain and quiet with a beautiful voice.

She sang The Beatles' *Eleanor Rigby* at the high school talent show. She wore a bland dress. The single spotlight illuminated a plain face made beautiful by her voice.

> *Eleanor Rigby died in the church and was buried along with her name.*
> *Nobody came*
> *Father McKenzie wiping the dirt from his hands as he walks from the grave*
> *No one was saved*
> *All the lonely people*

Where do they all come from?
All the lonely people
Where do they all belong?

Hazel's voice was thrilling. While she had possessed no hopes or ambition, she won the school competition.

The applause was chaotic and hot. It was then that Henry Issacs decided to take a shot.

He was cute and smart and rather sincere.

At the performance, he shed a tear.

Then he bought some beer.

Henry was excited by Hazel's prize and she was rather surprised by his inhibition.

They did not have to go far at all, only to the back of his messy car.

It was dark.

It was the night of an eclipse.

And she was a lonely girl who so wanted so to be kissed on the lips!

Hazel could not even believe that it

had happened!

It was so absurd.

She was so sure that the cloak of night would hide them forever.

When Music rises, Love surprises. The mask of night turned to dawn and developed waking eyes.

Hazel asked Henry what he was going to do about the absurdity besides shake in his shoes.

After all, these things happened in twos!

He was a good boy so he said he would drive her to the city.

Then, snap! Once again, she could be pretty.

She was unsure of what to do.

And she heard the Music call her name from the periwinkle blue.

Britney was beside herself.

She was singing and clapping and carrying on.

She was making as much noise as possible on the other side of the stars.

It sounded like a sea sick in guitars.

Whhaaaaahhhhhh!

Please, please help me!

She could still recall Maddie's heart ringing near. But she was in quivering fear!

Would she ever find her friend?

"Be patient, child!" The Music rang.

"But she will forget me."

"Do not worry, Britney. I am here here and I shall not forget."

And she stared out at the planets and gentle stars and the galaxies and became forlorn for she knew a special love.

The Universe is so large, just look at it! she cried.

"Believe," the Music sang.

Despite her parents' protestations, Hazel Hoppenfop had her own aspirations.

She could not bring herself to 'take care' of the baby.

"Darling, that child will ruin your life!"

"Well, she won't ruin mine. Besides, it's just for a while."

"Of all the guile! How can you be objective? You have no perspective! You're only sixteen!"

"And it's only another seven months!"

"Then if you won't do it for yourself, do it for me!" her mother whimpered.

"Do I not have a say in the matter?" Hazel simpered.

"No!"

"Mom, you need to lie down in your bed."

"For heaven's sake, I am wide awake! Just tell me."

Then Hazel stammered as she spoke. It was as if she had suddenly awoke.

"I can't fully explain. I hear a song. This child longs

to belong."

Well, Hazel thought that Henry was a weak little mouse. When she walked past him, he would hide his eyes like a louse.

Yet, even though he had dissed her, she could not help but think that he was still cute.

He wore that wonderful smile.

She was going to go that extra mile.

She thought the little baby , the little Henry-Hazel- Hoo, running bare feet in the wheat, would be ever such a treat.

Of course, so did Britney on the other side of the earth-treading stars.

So, in their small town with the clocktower in the square, Hazel let the baby grow.

It was just something she thought was right even though her parents frowned. Their anger became too much for her once she was at five months and glowing. So she decided to stop showing.

She sought calmer accommodations.

She stayed at a convent-school known as "Our Lady of the Woods." There she continued her high school education without trepidation. The old nuns were dying with no new ones applying so Hazel was a welcome guest.

Hazel had her own room for rest. The sisters were funny and pretty. They took no pity for all was love. For her music, she had her earphones and never created any strife in the quaint, monastic life.

She was struck by the beauty and devotion of the sisters' love. She realized that not all of us are destined for an earthly love, or earthly children in a home.

There are those who seek the divine romance, alone.

She understood and respected it, but she liked boys too much to take part in it.

Every morning, Hazel walked barefoot through the tree-lined paths and attended mass with the joyous nuns. She would wear long white skirts and coral tops. The nuns were never exhausting, just sweet, like frosting. Being in their gaggle allowed her to cope. In the unseen, she developed hope. She loved hanging with them. Unlike her parents who disliked the teen, the sisters had not one ounce of mean.

Despite the convent's woodsy land, the inside was very grand. The altar of worship looked like a great Faberge egg of sky blue and gold. It was founded by nuns from France which explains why you wanted to dance in a place such as this.

Reverence always precedes understanding. For Hazel, she came to the altar with a heart that was sincere and naked. She had great respect in worship of the Sacred.

Every time, Love pushed down the door where her loneliness lived.

The Music came and sealed the chamber of her heart.

She was filled with clear sweetness that was there from the start.

Well, she wasn't going to join the sisterhood once the baby was born! Still, she had found the Music that could not be shorn.

In the months to follow, her own life bore the fruit of a loving song.

There was tenderness, kindness, and no wrong.

She had but one request of the parents who would adopt her baby—

That the baby be raised in a family that loved Music.

Hazel was walking in the green woods of the convent when her water broke.

The green moss was soaked.

So, the Music shattered one short dream, allowing another song to rise.

Britney Anne was born a preemie.

She was all of eight months.

In her babyhood, so dreamy!

She could not wait to be born and begin her search for the one her heart loved.

Her red newborn face gave way to eyes that finally opened.

Britney had the eyes that all infants share when very young—the old eyes of the wise.

And then she began to bawl and coo. Later she began to walk as most children do.

Soon, she even learned how to tie her shoe.

As Britney Anne grew, those wise eyes disappeared into the eyes of a darling girl, and happiness which was once known in the secret land was gone from remembrance.

Time moved on, and she could not, would not, not now, possibly ever know Maddie's name.

Hazel Hoppenfop interviewed several couples and she fell in love with Rosalind and Joe Wilson.

The Wilsons emanated so much joy in them and they were forever laughing, appreciating one another. Joe worked a good job and could provide Britney with a good life. Their home in Noddingham, Ohio was filled with Love.

It was a love that was not a contract but an affection of the soul.

So baby Britney went home and joined the family.

At four years old, all appeared new, and strange

and inexpressibly rare to little Britney. The corn was golden and never seemed to be reaped nor even sown. All of life was a perpetual harvest. In this time, Rosalind, with her big flowered hats, taught Britney about the heart of Love—all knowing, faithful, beautiful and kind.

"You, my precious girl," her mother said, "you never need to worry."

"Why, mama?" said Britney.

"You are the apple of Love's eye."

It was true.

All of us are.

After all, are we not all lovelies?

And when she learned to read, Britney found this for herself, as well, as she immersed herself in the *Autobiography of Love* that rested on her mother's nightstand.

Britney's father, Joe, worked at the Corning glass factory and he would bring home glasses with small imperfections.

When Britney was old enough to leave her

sippy cup behind and drink from a real glass, her father gave her a gaily-colored children's glass for her morning juice.

It was all very grown up. A little orange bear, sat at a sunny table drinking from his juice glass. Britney loved that glass with all her heart. She would grow all tingly just seeing that work of art.

Then, an odd thing happened.

Britney put her finger on the ridge of the painted glass and rubbed it.

It made a perfect noise.

The kind of noise that goes on and on as a beautiful sound does once it has wrung the ear. It was the chord of the wild sea.

It was not long before Britney began to bring another glass and another glass to the table.

In a few short months, she was making a lovely melody with the only thing the Wilsons had at their home to make music - glasses.

It poured out from her home-made "glass harp".

"Why, that music gives me chills!" said Rosalind

Wilson. "It's absolutely heavenly!"

Joe would laugh his big hearty laugh as Britney ran her fingers over the water-filled glasses.

"She is our miracle baby!" he said.

"Our gift from Love!" Rosalind would chime in.

Something within the little girl seemed to dream in music. It made everything clean.

The music nursed the delicious ache.

It poured out from her with her "glass harp" that she made out of the dozens of irregular glasses that her Daddy brought home from the factory.

Where are you, oh heart, which I loved from the start?

Did you ever arrive?

How long must we stay apart?

One day returning home from kindergarten, Britney threw open the French windows in the living room. She wore a floral dress, tied with a bow.

A fresh spring wind blew through the house. She played a song on forty glasses.

The breeze carried the Music into the distant country plains, past the bullet trains, across the majestic cornfields and the Christmas tree farms.

The Music swept down the Georgia orange trees, the droning honeybees, and across the shining seas of the Atlantic.

It wafted past the London Pier.

Young Britney wanted all of Nod to hear.

Per chance or fate, there was someone who might be listening. Somewhere there was someone who would answer her musical dream.

They could play games and laugh together and they would be happy.

When she was seven years old, Britney played *O Come, O Come Emmanuel!* on her long table of glasses at the First Baptist Church. She was already a distinguished member of the church as she was the only white girl in the whole place. And her gift for song made her even more special.

"She is a Love Gift!" Rosalind would roar as she picked up her little cub so the Reverend could seal this bliss with a kiss upon Britney's sweet forehead.

Rosalind would bring home colored scarves on sale from department stores. As Britney played her glass harp, Rosalind would dance around the house waving the scarves dramatically as if she were Esmeralda, herself.

At the age of ten, Britney made the national news when she was invited to the Easter Celebration at St. Patrick's Cathedral in New York City.

There, she played Handel's *Hallelujah* on one hundred and twenty wine glasses. She spellbound crowds as well as the news who sat in the pews. It was a sound that astounded as it rounded ever curve in the cathedral.

It was as if Britney , in her long black skirt and yellow top, was summoning something, someone, and she was.

She was calling out to someone brave and nameless and soft.

Her music crossed the ocean white with foam.

However, Madeline Lauren Eaves could not hear

and was feeling very alone.

So the little girl, Britney, kept looking for a place to call home.

Maddie grew up in science. Her parents were delighted with her smoking volcano at year two in Infant School.

When Maddie was ten, she won the Junior school science fair. She did it with a convincing re-creation of the heart. It pumped crimson food coloring into a plastic human that was state of the art. It would have pleased even Descartes, a man of science, too, who believed while reality was showable it was completely unknowable.

Because she was a child of fact from biological parents, Maddie was encouraged in the discipline of the age.

Nod was changing fast and science was an

application that would give her a future of satisfaction.

Of course, with parents so bright, Maddie would certainly become a doctor, of the heart, perhaps. But she could not seem to cope with turning away from the telescope.

She kept looking at the evening star as if it was a luscious candy bar.

"But this is no fallacy! The body is like a galaxy!" Her father, the engineer, had told her.

He made her watch *Fantastic Voyage*, an old movie where people shrunk to the size of atoms so they could beam through the stratums. There, with Raquel Welch at the helm, they flew as a team through the blood stream. Finally, they came to the human heart which was bigger than any supermart.

No matter how delicious the movie popcorn, Maddie was not at all interested.

"It's just not for me, Daddy. "It's not my dream."

"But, buttonhead, there is so much yet to know."

"I like the real deal."

"The real deal. What is that?"

"The planets and stars…and the universe"

"I blame your mother for this."

"Don't blame, Mommy."

"I may have a fit! Why didn't we get you a doctor's kit? What a dope! Buying you that damn telescope. Seven years old is a formative time! Now all I can do is whine! "

"But, Daddy, there is so much to explore out there - nothing even compares!"

Maddie went to the window and looked out at the night sky dripping in shiny stars.

"Doctors are something that Nod needs. I cannot say the same for astronomers."

Maddie calmed her father. She was twelve and spry. "Don't worry Daddy, I'll get by."

And so Maddie's dad sucked it up. After all, he was a forward-thinking man. He thought he could write the perfect book for his daughter.

But that night, he realized that he could only turn

the pages for her.

She would be what she would be.

So he jumped into her world of sky. He would give it a try! No lab lamp! Instead, space camp! There, Maddie learned to walk in pods without the pull of gravity.

For all the science, Maddie received little training in matters of the heart. So she was smart, but miles apart from her soul.

While her friends started dating, she continued to look at the numerous stars as if the distant dream would somehow be discovered.

She withdrew into herself with this secret loneliness. The need to succeed from her parents overwhelmed her. To shield her eyes from Nod, she wore eyeglasses to hide her face. She did not want to be part of this race.

Meanwhile, Britney's appearance at Saint Patrick's, prompted a Florida casting agent to come to Noddingham. He offered her parents a long-term contract for Britney. She would sing and dance with other teens under spotlight beams. The address of such egress was known as "The Magic Kingdom".

Britney moved to Florida with her parents to acquire television knowledge, while Maddie started college.

Maddie was a brilliant student. So it was incongruous that she would start drinking. In her eyeglasses and prudish dress, she seemed repressed. But she would go to a bar in London and would transgress.

She did not know what was truly going on. She just knew that when she saw *Doctor Zhivago* on late night telly, she rather liked Lara's fury over the poetry of Yuri.

Since Maddie could no longer trust herself to know who she was, she allowed drink to inhabit her lust and tear her to dust.

And Daddy science would not approve of playing doctor with the nurses…*except perhaps, there was still hope of finding a respectable job!*

Maddie drank on Saturday night so she could be alone in bed with someone else on Sunday morning.

But was there any fault in the stars? Was she not meant for love, for meaning? But love – it can neither possess nor can it be possessed. For in the giving, the more one has, the more one gives. Love cannot be bound for Love is infinite, moving past beyond the beginning and the end.

But Love - oh, what a friend! Love never returns, nor departs. Love is forever there in each of our hearts.

Oh Love, maker of mercy and kindness!

Show yourself to me!

Love, please! Love find me!

As much as science had aided her birth, now as a woman, Maddie could find no solace. The magic men in their magic white coats who told the Nods how to feel and deal, were often as empty as straw. In her suffering and pain, she grew raw. A utopian vision of machine people in perfect harmony seemed empty of poetry, music and art. Through the power of science, she could reach anyone at anytime around the world but no one seemed to know what to say.

The mystery of the Universe which she had studied, dwarfed her. For a woman as fit as she, the mystery morphed her. She could not even lift the spoon of her cereal bowl.

The days of summer with their glimmering enchantment of dancing ladybugs and sailing clouds had faded into grey. Maddie's heart had somehow faded along with it.

We all have our gifts that are given to us before we are born.

That is our fate.

Our destiny is to use or abuse them.

Drink became Maddie's favorite friend. It did not require her to laugh or smile or tell enchanting stories to keep friendship alive.

She did not seek joy or courage in drink, only to forget herself in the intoxication, nothing more, nothing less.

She became the bad company that she kept, losing herself as she wept.

And the disordering darkness moved into her heart and shattered it.

She was sick of her feet and her hands and her face.

She grew tired of running in the human race.

In those days, the one tear she shed was as big as the sea, and in the waves, she nearly drowned.

She found herself staring down from the 45th floor of her apartment building.

The window of her loneliness would become her exit.

Within a few weeks, the would-be astronomer had opened the window to throw herself out.

This could be a new life, free of strife.

The wind was forceful that three am.

At the open window, she found herself fighting against it.

Then, she heard the Music call her name.

"Do you not recall me?" The winged heart sang.

Maddie was puzzled at the open window.

I don't remember.

"Did I not ask you to call for me?"

When?

"In the twinkle."

I don't know.

"Yes, that is the way it often is. But I called your name and you did not come."

"Well, here you are." Maddie said. "Now what do you want?"

"I want you to call me into your soul. I will give you strength to withstand all of this."

"Are you Love?"

"Yes, I am Love."

"I have science," Maddie said.

"I am also science," said the Music. "Science is but an aspect of Me. I love you and I desire you to love me. When you believe, I will come."

You will live within me? You will stop the pain?

"Yes, Maddie. Why choose the darkness when you can have the light? I will guide your gifts and make you strong because I love you."

"Where have you been all my life?"

"Playing inside your heart. I have been there from the start."

Maddie's heart broke loose with the Music.

"Oh come, though you have broken your promises a hundred times…come home, stranger and alien, come home to me….come home, space traveler, lover of leaving, for I am here..."

In that moment, Maddie closed the window on the 45th floor and let Love into her heart.

The next day, Maddie walked the streets of London, Nod.

Love came along.

So let me get this straight. The Kingdom of Love is within me?

"Yes. Isn't that remarkable?"

And you will help me?

"I shall. I made the galaxies. I can certainly help you whom I love."

But the galaxies are science.

"All science came from me."

"Sorry…" Maddie said. "I keep forgetting."

And so Maddie did what so many had done before her, she carried a new Love within and braced herself like a hero.

*T***here is a river** *whose streams make glad the city of Love.*

Along that river is the tree of Heaven.

For it, there is no beginning.

It is holy and beautiful and never-ending.

It is large and unknowable.

For there are secret things that belong only to Love.

The holy music worked through Maddie in the months to come.

She became the virtues embodied in the stories of women she revered, people like Joan of Arc, Hester Prynne, Teresa of Avila, and Eleanor Roosevelt.

Maddie often went for a drive to Jade Spring Mountain on the outskirts of London, Nod. She especially enjoyed sitting in a little garden filled with lotus flowers known as "The Pure Heart Garden" grown in honor of an ancient Emperor. The crystalline waters reflected all the myriad colors of nature. In the river swam the gleaming fish, which were meant for water just as humankind is meant for love.

Sometimes she would be at the springs by night and find fortune. This pilgrim went to be near the water but instead found the reflection of the moon.

Her dreams were no longer children of the idle heart but of the sincere heart.

She had a new look that came not merely from a book.

"Any color, any shape, any size, may the dream come for the true and only one," she prayed.

The Light of Love was delighted to oblige.

For the Love you seek shall show you surprises!

And no foundation in Nod shall stop Love.

For skyscrapers shall fall while the Music rises.

Even amidst the shadows and threat of thunder, remains the light and awe of wonder!

Her music was a sensation. The television series launched her brilliant star. Britney Wilson was both lovely and wholesome. That fragile song of glasses ringing as a child had crescendoed into the voice of a young woman.

When she sang, Britney sang like the mocking-birds, not worrying about who would hear her or what they would think. The fearless songs that she wrote touched the heart of her generation.

Britney's passion against the machine seemed to captivate her generation as Huck Finn or Holden Caulfield had captivated their own. She wanted what all young people wanted. To be true and real and not conform.

Her song, *We Will Sing*, became an anthem for teens across Nod. The song proposed a brave life which rebelled against the hypocrisy of the old grey land, which was fed by materialism, not love; ego, not community.

Britney made it a point to spend an hour with her fans before every concert. She would sign every autograph and help, when she could, with any answer.

Rosalind and Joe Wilson were proud of their daughter. They loved the songs she wrote – they were rebellious as youth tend to be. The lyrics spoke of the unseen possibilities of compassion. And even Hazel Hoppenfop was thankful as she saw her own talents shine in Britney from afar.

Hazel had swapped her plain dress for a colorful closet of dresses. She ran the local community theatre where she would sing from time to time. She was married and over a span of ten years, had five boys.

It was Rosalind Wilson who invited Hazel back into Britney's life. In fact, when Britney was playing a stadium in Cleveland Ohio, Rosalind had arranged for

Britney to meet her biological mother.

They had a lovely lunch.

West Side Story, really?" Britney asked.

"Yes," laughed Hazel.

"I love that musical. Stephen Sondheim is my favorite lyricist!" said Britney.

The two women were giddy in their shared love for musical theatre.

There's a place for us,
Somewhere a place for us. Hazel sang.

With glee, Britney glided into a duet….

Peace and quiet and open air
Wait for us …
Somewhere!

The Music broke down all consideration and Britney hugged Hazel with affection.

"What a lovely voice you have!" Britney enthused.

Hazel began to cry.

Her voice had become Britney's voice.

"Oh come tonight! Come sing a duet with me." Britney pleaded. " I'll have the band learn the song. It would make me so happy."

"Really?" said Hazel. " That would be a dream come true to sing with you!"

That summer's night, with Hazel's husband, Leo, and her five boys sitting in the front row and with Rosalind and Joe Wilson beside them, the two women stood on the center stage of the Cleveland Indians stadium.

"I have always loved this next song written by Leonard Bernstein and Stephen Sondheim. There is such optimism in it. Tonight, it is especially unique for my biological Mom and I are going to sing this. My real mom, Rosalind is here as well to enjoy it."

Britney looked out past the lights for her mother and spotted her in the house seats.

"Stand up, Mom, let everyone see you." Rosalind stood and waved proudly. Never sheepish about anything, she turned around and waved to the entire crowd, bowing profusely in a chiffon cloud of purple flowers.

Hazel came onto the stage in her navy blue satin gown. There was no plain dress in which she could frown.

For the first time ever, Hazel was in a fright even on this special night.

But her daughter looked into her eyes, what a surprise.

Then, she was ready.

Mother and daughter took each other's hand. They sang the song from *West Side Story*—

> *There's a time for us,*
> *Some day a time for us,*
> *Time together with time spare,*
> *Time to learn, time to care,*
> *Some day!*
>
> *Somewhere.*
> *We'll find a new way of living,*
> *We'll find a way of forgiving*
> *Somewhere.*
>
> *There's a place for us,*
> *A time and place for us.*

Hold my hand and we're halfway there.
Hold my hand and I'll take you there
Somehow,
Some day,
Somewhere!

As they took a bow to thundering applause, Britney and Hazel clasped hands. They were surprised. They were pretty good, but...

What was it? Britney needed to ponder the wonder of this musical thunder.

It was the inexplicable power of family voices in harmony – there was a mystery always in the harmony of biological voices. Whether it be the Von Trapp Singers or the Jackson Five...

To Britney's surprise, the applause did not stop. The two young women brought their hands together in one heart.

The audience went wild.

When Britney waved her mother to stand, Rosalind did -- never one to hide.

The entire stadium stood and cheered.

Britney thought it strange. Certainly this was no flop.

Then it became clear—Rosalind, Britney and Hazel, separate and different yet together, forever through Love.

They were applauding the crazy quilt of family.

That *Somewhere* duet had somehow closed a chapter of Britney's life that night. This was the year of her high school graduation. Britney decided not to continue as a teen star writing teeny-bopper songs of love anymore.

She was looking for something more.

With her fair according voice, Britney made a choice.

With her parents' blessing, she enrolled in Julliard and started a new life.

Some way. Somewhere. Some place.

There were many boys at Julliard who conquered the intimidation of her celebrity and summoned the courage to ask Britney out on a date. There were artistic and serious guys at university, largely musicians and singers, but they were… *sooo* serious. None displeased, but she did not grow weak in the knees.

Why dream and wait for you any longer?

She prayed for the door to open to the love of her dreams. Someone kind, who yearned to do what was right, who was strong and who could laugh in the corridor of light. Her soul insisted there existed the one, although her mind was dim to it.

She wandered mazily in her dreams, asking *Will*

you come back? Will you leave me here, dying?

"Mama?"

"What is it, honey?"

"For years, I have been writing about *him*."

"Don't worry, honey. You'll find him. There is someone special for each of us."

"But what if it is a *her*?"

"Oh."

Rosalind looked over at Britney, her jaw unhinged. Her eyes filled with tears and her mouth chattered as if she was freezing cold.

"I have been making so much money, Mama, by writing *him* instead of *her*."

"I see."

"I think it's always been that way, Mama."

"Darling."

And Rosalind took her daughter into her arms.

"What should I do, Mama?"

Then Rosalind prayed. The clouds were all around her. What was pure? What was holy? And what was right? The fullness of Music fell on her like soft rain.

"Then you must find her."

"Find her?"

"We are not happy, Britney, because of anything but love. It is not that we pursue happiness. We are happy because we pursue love. There is but one commandment, Britney - to love."

"Mama…"

Britney sobbed in her mother's arms.

"And when you find her, love her with all your heart."

"Mama…"

"Look in every city or any town. Travel by foot, or train or plane. Do not settle until there is love. For there will be the address of your happiness."

"But?"

"There is no but, Britney. All things are possible

with Love."

"Yes, Mama."

"I love you, baby."

"I love you, too, Mama."

Grey is the color that always seems on the eve of changing, of brightening into blue or blanching into white.

So Britney would pray in those grey mornings with the hope that persists amidst the doubt.

In the summers from Julliard, she traveled on mission trips.

She looked in houses, huts, skylines, mountains, lighthouses and the sea. At night, she searched in the land blanketed by her dreams.

She wandered through forests, palm trees, amidst maples scarlet with Ohio autumn, and Central Park elms so new in spring that their green was almost white.

Like the songs that she grew up on, this lovely pilgrim saw the blue at the end of *the rainbow*, she knew that *somewhere there was a place for her in Nod*.

Maddie did not see her. Still, she loved her blindly.

But this love was not a bond, rather it moved like the sea between the shores of two souls.

She went here.

She went there.

She looked everywhere.

But she could not find her.

Yet, happy are the pure of heart for they have known the Music.

Somewhere outside of Hong Kong, Maddie and Britney were on the same train, their eyes cast in the same direction.

Maddie was in car four.

Britney was in car five.

It was 11 am when Britney felt the stirring.

Suddenly, as if arrested by fear or a feeling of wonder, Britney stood with her colorless lips apart.

Let go, dance without feet.

A shudder ran through her frame, compelling her to leave the train car.

As Britney pushed up the stairs of the crowded underground station, she glimpsed a distant figure.

It had to be her, yes, it was her!

For a moment, her heart leapt.

She hurried up the steps but the figure was lost in the crush of the city.

She stopped on the pavement, wounded by her vanishing scent.

You never know who the stranger next to you could be.

Watch, knock, seek….

…*Find me!*

The winged heart works in miraculous ways. The Music blows wherever Music pleases, you hear it's sound, but you cannot tell where the Music comes from or where the Music is going.

Music rises like daydreams.

So Maddie and Britney looked for one another over the great blue marble of Nod, driven by the delicious ache inspired by the Kingdom within.

Be of good cheer, follow the fugitive lover.

Maddie was in New Delhi at a science conference. She was an in-demand speaker in the world of astronomy as there were few people on Nod who knew the stars as she did.

It was in India when she got the call.

It was her agent for speaking engagements.

"NASA would like you to introduce this space thing-a-ma-jig at the Kennedy Center."

"What exactly is it?"

"It's Imax-type footage of the universe set to music, including everything from the cell to the Milky Way."

"What do you think?"

"It's an important piece. The President will be there. And your schedule is free."

"Sounds good to me."

"Oh yeah, and one other thing, the music was written by that teen phenom in the states."

"Who?"

"Britney Wilson."

"I don't know who that is."

"That's because you're a Brit. Well, she's no longer a teen. She went off to Julliard and wrote this thing-a-ma-jig."

"The thing-a-ma-jig?"

"Oh, Maddie, it's big. I'm surprised you haven't heard of it. It's about the Kingdom of Love. It's called, *The Address of Happiness*."

There had been a storm in Washington DC and Maddie's plane was late. Maddie was always late. The driver who picked her up at Reagan said that with a little luck, they might just make it in time for her to give the introduction.

With her overcoat flying, her umbrella blown backward against the wind, she came into the stage entrance of the Kennedy Center. She combed back her wet hair and adjusted her elegant outfit. She wore a black shirt with black skirt, lace tights, and red heels.

Composed, she took the stage flooded by applause.

Maddie spoke on the importance of continuing scientific endeavors. She talked of how the "Sender" was sending a message to all of us about life. Part of the journey of life was to find out what the message was.

"For through that journey, we come to learn the beauty and majesty of that message.

"Britney Anne Wilson has searched all her life for the place of happiness," Maddie said. "I admire anyone who forsakes success to test herself with new horizons. An award-winning singer and song-writer at an early age, Britney surprised the world by giving up a career for the pursuit of higher education at the Julliard Academy. Now at the age of twenty four, Britney returns with her symphony that posits the idea that happiness can be found at the very center of ourselves when we truly love another."

Britney's throat tightened as Maddie spoke. Her mouth went dry as she listened to the voice from backstage. It was a memorable voice, one of clarity and strength, but also possessed of softness. Britney trembled with the sound of it. It stirred the sad ache that was written on her heart from the very start.

With that, the lights dimmed. Maddie, per the

written stage directions on the podium, exited the stage.

She strolled to the back of the first floor of the Kennedy center.

Out of the dark and silent stage, Britney rose from the conductor's well on a hydrolift. She bowed to the audience who greeted her with hearty applause.

From the back of the theatre, Maddie could see that she was attractive. Her hair shone like a halo beneath the spotlight.

She wore a sequined black dress with patent-leather heels with her long hair tied back. Around her neck was a simple silver cross which she had found at a jewelry shop in New Mexico, Nod while looking for her love of loves. She had the look of a young Audrey Hepburn, an actress from the 20th century who had once said, *For beautiful eyes, look for the good in others; for beautiful lips, speak only words of kindness; and for poise, walk with the knowledge that you are never alone.*

What stirred Maddie was not necessarily Britney's beauty. Oh yes, she was lovely, all right.

There was something else.

As the lights dimmed again, and the violins swelled, she heard in the preamble a melody that somehow, somewhere she had known.

The screens behind the orchestra came alive with imagery.

The music was soft at first as the light moved over the sea. It grew louder and bigger as creation unfolded. The planets and galaxies were born into the light.

The screen moved in on a cell. The close-up revealed a city inside the cell's nucleus as complex and intricate as any modern Aerotropolis.

The music soared and was, itself, as memorable as the work of Gustav Holst's *The Planets*.

Britney had written the hour and half piece of music in a record, twelve days, shorter than Handel who, too, had been seized by the Spirit. Handel wrote a whopping four hours of the *The Messiah* in only twenty one days, including the full orchestrations.

It does speak to the miracle of the Music which makes souls pure.

Madeline Lauren Eaves stood there at the back of the massive theatre, slack-jawed. She thought the music and photography was the most beautiful confluence of sound and imagery she had ever seen.

Once again, she was a seven-year-old staring out at the mystery of tender stars.

That night, Britney sensed as well a different presence in the theatre. It was the very presence of Majestic Music.

An answer had come to her soul and she shivered from head to toe.

Then a strange thing happened, the very music that she had written ravished her.

She played the baton to the 120-piece orchestra with energy beyond her own.

The room became alive with Love.

Two who were bitter, were enriched with restored love. They remembered all that had been good between them.

A new couple tenderly took one another's hands for the first time.

The crowd was astounded. It was not just the music. It was something much more and they all experienced it. They were a society now of the Burning Heart, children of the Deeper Life.

Yes, it was supernatural.

And Love is the weaver of the sacred thread and the tapestry for Love's loom is the universe.

The standing ovation brought three curtain calls. The crowd loved Britney from where she had come and loved her even more for where she was going. Finally Britney put down her conductor's baton and sang for the audience the song that the symphony was named for - *The Address Of Happiness*.

Following the encore, the audience rushed past the immoveable Maddie who stood at the back of the theatre.

There was something about that voice.

Maddie had to meet the woman she had introduced.

She wanted to thank her for a job well done or so she thought.

With a beating heart and a nervousness she could not understand, she walked against the crowd to the backstage.

The orchestra was packing up their instruments. Some band members engaged in cheerful chit chat.

Her stomach ached.

She had met many famous and highly regarded people. But she had never met anyone who spoke to her heart like Britney.

Her heart kept beating louder. There was a strong and distant hand upon her music, something that seemed to deeply pull at her soul. Perhaps that is why her heart beat so.

Maddie walked down the long corridor of beige dressing rooms.

At the end of the wall was a guard and some baskets of flowers, scattered here and there on the linoleum tiled floor.

"Is it alright if I knock?" she asked the guard.

"Yes, of course." He said with a heavenly smile. His eyes had a tender twinkle. They were the color of periwinkle.

She summoned her gumption and knocked.

The door was painted white.

"Come in" Britney said.

Then Maddie entered.

And Britney turned.

Then she saw her.

Something swelled both their hearts.

The whole of love fell upon them.

Britney stood up, not knowing why she was smiling.

Maddie came to her.

They found themselves in each other's eyes.

In an inexplicable gesture, Britney opened her arms to her.

The woman of her dreams went into her arms without shame or awkwardness as the boldness of Love overcame them both.

It was as if they had known each other forever.

Love is what we are born into.

Fear is what we learn.

Love is what we must return to if our lives are to have any meaning.

For we were born for meaning.

We were born for love.

And in the weeks ahead, they would trace the map of happiness together – on runways, roads, streets and paths.

Where they had once wandered alone, they now walked together home.

Oft, they sauntered forward in silence, basking in the mystery of it all.

They strolled the old country road of Nodding-ham where Britney had been born. There, the maples and elm, once again, were bursting with autumn color.

There they were walking together in the same direction, holding hands.

That's what Love can do.

Love makes it better.

Love makes everything better.

It was a white wedding. They were married in Paris, Nod in the new planetarium. Britney had always loved the idea of Paris. The planetarium was filled with white lotus flowers and lavender forget-me-nots, swirling with huge screens of the planets and the earth treading stars. The wedding cake, a tower of cupcakes, was meant to resemble the Eiffel tower, the symbol of the city.

Maddie, who was perpetually late, was early.

Pastor Washington from the First Baptist Church of Britney's small town presided. The Pastor had never been to Europe before and it was a thrilling third honeymoon for him and his wife.

"Oh brothers and sisters, today we celebrate under this sacred union between Britney Anne Wilson and Maddie Lauren Eaves."

The brides never looked so beautiful. Rosalind Wilson had made the dresses herself, laden with white lace and crowned with veils of pearls.

The pearls were like breaking stars across the face carefully sewn with an unseen trace.

When Maddie lifted the veil from Britney's face, she was overcome.

Britney was the first and only one.

She saw the scarlet thread of her lips, the light in her eyes, the family through their love, their children running barefoot in a fresh field.

She knew at once her tenderness and the strength of her.

She was hers, neither a passenger nor driver.

Maddie's dream was cupped in Britney's dream.

It was a dream that was not temporal, but eternal.

It was a dream not of leaving but of staying.

...so said the Music.

"Maddie, do you take Britney for your lawful wedded wife, to live in the holy estate of matrimony? Will you love, honor, comfort, and cherish her from this day forward, forsaking all others, keeping only unto her for as long as you both shall live?"

"I do."

Elaine and Ben Eaves elected not to attend. Joe danced with his Britney and then with her bride.

"I hope you know how much I love you," Joe told Maddie.

Her eyes turned up in wonder.

She had been a stranger for a long time. She could stop traveling.

There was the thunder of her heart cracking.

She put her head on her father-in-law's shoulder.

And like all brides on the day, she cried all over again.

Rosalind sang a "Hallelujah!" as she swept off her big flowered hat as if it was her last chance to dance.

Joe Wilson formed a Mississippi Mudslide line so

everyone could celebrate the romance.

And the wedding party of parties began.

Later, as the sky tarnished to the color of rose that rests inside the seashell, the wedding couple rode a bicycle down the sidewalk of Avenue des Champs-Élysées beneath the chestnut trees.

"I love you," said Maddie.

"I love you," replied Britney.

Their wedding night was at a little hotel in Paris. There were walk up steps and a lovely view and all was well for these two.

In the garden, in the making of bread, in the loving, and in the struggle, it all seemed a miracle. In Nod, there were times for everything under Heaven.

There was time to dance. Time to laugh. Time to cry. Time to arise and shine. In love, Maddie watched her bride's pale arms take the rolling pin over the pastry dough; her hands guide her brush of crushed shells through her lush hair; her fingers in prayer, petitioning.

In the ordinary life, they found the mystical ascent that comes from walking with Music.

They learned to live contently with small things, to seek elegance rather than luxury, and refinement rather than fashion, to be worthy not respectable, and to be rich not wealthy. They let the sacred and unconscious bloom amidst the common, rendering it all extraordinary.

Comfort never became a repression in their home, for the passion of the soul was always churning, making everything pure again.

It only took a few minutes for the two brides to be married, but in the rough and tumble of a home, it would take years for Britney and Maddie's love to dovetail into one love.

They were two hands holding one heart.

True love is always observant.

It knows the need.

So together they found the love that was true.

They lived in the sweet world.

For Love makes even the sorrows sweet.

Sometimes there were troubles but no one can be a hero without the heart being torn open.

There was no necessity for either to have the last word.

For the first word became the only word of their

romantic conversation.

There were spaces in their togetherness, and fire in their aloneness.

And when they would return to one another from their solitude, they returned gently as dew comes to the morning grass.

Oh, there were differences and there was heat, for they were human after-all, but they had been touched with the Music which always nurtures, always encourages, that forever soothes the pain. The differences never lasted. Rather, they spun out into the air neither resting nor rooting in either soul.

For human beings must be served, not exploited, honored, not manipulated.

The marriage bond is more than a civil contract.

It is a reward for loving well.

For happy are the merciful for they shall, too, know mercy; and happy are the pure of heart for they shall hear the Music.

Baby Matthew came after their first year of marriage.

The adoption agency had been so helpful.

He was pink and feisty, and like Maddie, he really did not seem very comfortable being born.

Matt had kicked and screamed trying to climb back to the secret place for he had met someone very special—a soul known as "Emma".

So like his mother Maddie, Matt was born almost a full month late.

He cried and cried, wanting to go back.

But he could not go back. He was pressing forward. He was to go through the kiln of Nod, where perfection is rendered through the days.

Baby Lily came three years later.

She was a preemie and seemed very content to be born early so she could get busy and run the race of life, thank you very much.

"Mama, I want to learn the music on the glasses," Lily said at age three to mother Britney.

"When you are old enough, honey, we'll make sure of it."

"Oh, Mama, will you cross your heart and hope to die?"

"I promise, Lily." And she crossed her heart.

The farmlands of the American Midwest lifted little Lily's Spirit. She jumped like the frogs. She moved like the birds in flight. As her mother Britney, had known before her, the corn of the fields appeared immortal and golden.

When she was five, Lily asked for some vegetable and flower seeds for her birthday.

Her mothers, of course, obliged and Lily was presented a basket of colorful envelopes. She studied the orange, yellow, red and greens. And she looked at the royal blue on the envelope containing the seeds of the forget-me-nots.

In a bit of earth in the backyard, Britney and Lily planted the seeds, row by row.

There were tomato, bean, and onions seeds as well as daisies.

"Gently," Britney said as Lily made holes in the soil and placed single tomato seeds into them.

"Softly," Britney advised as Lily tenderly sealed the seeds with a layer of the good earth.

Patience and optimism brings order to the life of any child. Good love is the love of order.

In May and June, Lily watered the seedlings every morning. The sun rose every day. It was the same sun that shown on all those solid soldiers of Nod through the epic arc of their lives.

The garden grew. By mid summer, there was much to harvest.

Maddie and Lily prepared green salads for meals, and cut vases of flowers for the kitchen.

"I think those are the prettiest flowers that I have ever seen!" Britney would say looking at the blue for-get-me-nots on the white kitchen table.

"Oh, Mommy!" Lily would cry. "It's like magic!"

"But it's not magic!," Maddie would laugh.

"Yes," Lily would reply. "It's not magic, Mommy! It's a-maz-ing!"

And in the fall, the cold would wither that which was known, scattering new seed.

In the spring, that which had been sleeping awoke and a new season of beauty began.

For Life seeks life and builds a bridge across the darkest valley.

Matt was curious and lyrical and so Maddie and Britney encouraged him as such.

He was anxious to let his mothers know about his discoveries in Nod.

He watched the universe through Maddie's telescope from so many birthdays ago.

"In the clouds today there was a space ship, a dinosaur, and an orangutan," he would say with confidence.

"That's lovely," Maddie sighed.

"And tomorrow, I am hoping that I will see the skyline of Kathmandu!"

He loved words and images. From the beginning, Britney would read Dr. Seuss to him; and before he went into first grade, Matt knew every book by heart. Of course, he knew *all the places he would go*. He was always eager to put on a show.

He tossed a word like a ball, never letting it fall. Instead it swam in the air, without care, strung together with an art that came straight from his heart. So early on, he began to make word games in the living room. His neighborhood friends would clap to his rap.

"Slow down, son," Britney would gently say. For parenting in its simplest form was patience….even with cadence!

"I am slowing down, Mom."

"Put the picture in your head and describe what you see instead."

And over time, mother and son worked together to perfect the boy's lyrical skills.

Lily had a voice like Britney which was a bit strange, and, oh my, what a range!

At an early age, Lily joined the church choir. Lily went through every page of the hymnal, practicing every song until her voice was fire. The very tree of heaven within her grew as her voice lifted to the clouds, touching the spaceships and orangutans.

One night, as the summer fireflies brightened the sky outside their bedroom window, Britney turned to Maddie.

"Why?" Britney asked. "Why all this?"

"Love cannot be love unless we choose it."

"And if we don't chose it?"

"Then we have not fulfilled what we were meant to do—to love."

"And the ups and the downs?"

"Well, let me think," she said as she watched the fireflies float against the window screen.

"The ups and downs…."

"Yes, those ups and downs…" she smiled.

"They make love stronger."

"Hmmm."

"Without the scrape, there is no scar."

"I could live without the scars."

"But that's where the music is."

"Hmmm." She said as she took her hand in hers

and squeezed it.

And she looked over.

Maddie was already asleep, her caring and generous eyes had closed in a dream.

The locusts had started. They were all around in every tree so that their music seemed to come from nowhere and everywhere at once.

Then there was the stillness except for the frogs flopping in the cooling grass of the backyard.

Soon Britney, too, dreamed.

She dreamed of how a hero comes to be.

Heroes do not dwell in a time of peace. Heroes are hardened in a kiln against the sorrows. Their troubles sharpen the blade and make it gleaming. The glint becomes a brightness that is raised high on a hill, allowing women and men to see beyond themselves. For light swallows darkness. Truth buries death. Heroes are not born. They are filled by Music.

The dream of life is the incredible struggle.

Today, we live. Tomorrow is uncertain.

Love is the reason why, even in suffering, we smile.

In confusion, we understand.

There will always be trouble in Nod so there will always be a time for heroes.

Britney was killed in a car accident with Rosalind and Joe Wilson that next day.

The three of them were coming back from the grocery store with burgers and buns for the 4th of July BBQ. A driver who had too much to drink collided straight into their van. Rosalind, Joe and Britney, along with the drunk driver, instantly departed.

Britney was only thirty-two years of age. She had barely turned her title page.

It was a large funeral. The First Lady was there. The Emperor of China stood at her grave in a robe beyond compare. Britney's symphony, *The Address of Happiness* had become an international treasure. Parts of the symphony were played and everyone stayed even when the music stopped.

As people left the cemetery, Maddie looked up from the children to see a lone figure standing in the distance.

Hazel took Matt and Lilly to the town car as Maddie walked towards the figure.

It was her mother.

She stood under a lone elm tree, far from the grave. Elaine Eaves was small to begin with, now even tinier in the shadow of the great elm.

Maddie came closer.

She looked into her eyes. Her lids twitched with pain.

"I am sorry for your loss," Elaine said quietly.

"Thank you."

"I am sorry for everything, Maddie."

"I know, Mama."

"If only…"

"It's alright, Mama.

Maddie saw the pain in her mother's left eye swell with a tear.

It broke from her eye and went down her cheek.

"Welcome home, Mama. Come, meet your grandchildren."

Elaine exploded into a sob.

She grabbed her daughter and the two of them became one in the convulsion.

Tears are another river that takes us home.

We become alive with tears.

There isn't a chance to return to sleep when we are weeping.

Maddie raised their children the best she could. She prayed on her knees every night that she might have the sensitivity of Britney.

Lily was a lovely girl. Matt was a happy boy.

They were the lovelies .

The apples of so many eyes.

Maddie would wake the children every morning, not by tearing away their blankets but by gently stroking their heads.

Maddie was there for the oatmeal.

She was there for the ballet recitals

She was there for the football games.

Most importantly, she was there with patience.

She showed up.

She loved them with a love that was never-ending.

So Matt and Lily grew as shining stars under the love of two mothers - one gone, hidden but not absent.

Maddie was so busy making sure that the children were healthy that she did not watch herself as carefully.

The pancreatic cancer spread quickly as it always does.

There was little that she could do but be brave for the family, and find yet another mother for the lovelies.

She asked Hazel Hoppenfop if she would finish raising the children.

Hazel looked at Maddie with sad eyes.

How had this all started?

On a night so long ago when Hazel sang, *Eleanor Rigby…*

All the lonely people
Where do they all come from?
All the lonely people
Where do they all belong?

Hazel's days on Nod had been so enriched by Britney and Maddie.

"I would do anything for you," she told Maddie. "It would be my honor."

Just as we take a train to get to Beijing or Manhattan, we take death to reach a star.

We cannot get to those tender constellations while we are alive any more than we can take the train when we are dead. Cancer, terrible cancer, is the celestial means of locomotion. Just as buses and railways are the terrestrial means.

To die quietly of old age would be to go to the stars on foot.

So for Maddie, she traveled to the stars not by foot but by a silver bullet train with her children and loved ones near.

She passed away at three in the morning with

Matt and Lily by her side.

In her sleep, she drifted slowly, past the land of ups and downs.

Past the angels and Mars, she floated into the gleam of the farthest stars.

Hazel Hoppenfop Higgins was a wonderful mom. She had raised five boys, after all.

"It will be alright," she told Lily and Matthew. "It will be different, but it will be alright."

"Yes, mam." Lily said.

Hazel stood on the front porch of the Britney and Maddie's home in Noddingham.

The two children were moving their things to a new world.

Hazel helped Lily and Matt take their boxes into the van that was hitched to her Suburban.

Matt had packed his socks and t-shirts into his mother's old book-bag which she took on speaking engagements. Matt could smell his mother Maddie's perfume on the bag. He was hoping that it would rub off on his t-shirts. The bag was so much bigger than he as he dragged it down the stairs to the car.

Matt was a good boy. He remained strong in the world. But when alone, he cried. He did not cry because it was over. He cried because it had begun - what we call 'love'. For in the sorrow, there is also our happiness. Memory wrecks us and ravishes us. It is sweet and stings and sustains us.

"I have one last thing," Lily said. "I need to go up to the attic. Is that okay?"

"Sure, honey. Do you need help?" asked Hazel.

"I've got it," the six year old said.

Matt was already in the front seat of the Suburban when Lily climbed down the steps.

She was carrying a tattered cardboard box that had been re-used so many times that there were a dozen different colored tapes on it.

"What is it, Lily?"

She placed the brown box on the white porch floor and opened it. There were several imperfect glasses in tissue and newspaper in the box.

"This is Mommy's glass harp, when she first learned the music."

Hazel looked at the ordinary juice glasses and drinking glasses. She picked up the glass with the orange teddy bear stretching to the morning sun.

"Oh, how beautiful."

"Yes. Mommy was worried I'd cut my fingers and I should wait 'til I was older to learn."

"I see."

"Do you think I'm older now? Could you teach me when we get to your house?"

"Yes, of course, Lily."

"Thank you, mam."

For Love promises to restore that which the locusts have eaten.

We must only believe.

As teenagers, Matt and Lily traveled with Hazel and her husband to the Lincoln Center.

This was the twenty fifth Anniversary event of *The Address Of Happiness.*

It had been that long since the debut at Julliard when Britney was only twenty two.

Matthew Wilson Eaves introduced the program.

He was nervous and fumbled with his tie. After all, courage is not the absence of fear. Courage is a determination that there is something *more important* than fear.

So at twenty one, Matt nervously pushed through his anxiousness.

He kept picturing what he wanted to say in his

mind, just like his mother Britney had taught him.

"In all the recitals I ever made to my two moms, they seemed to like this ditty the best. My mother Britney was a lyricist, my mother Maddie tried to keep up with her. My mom Britney helped me write this. I first delivered it from a pup tent in the backyard at the age of seven."

As on cue, the screens on the stage came alive with the fantastic cities of life—the life in the nucleus of the human cell, in the blade of grass, in the energy of a kiss, and in stars colliding.

"So with great affection towards my two mothers and to all the folks they have touched, I present the poem, *Pour!* written by Britney Anne Wilson and me."

He spoke gently and straightforwardly—

Here, soul meets soul,
Here, heart in heart pours,
The Music has no body but yours,
No hands, no feet on earth but yours.

Yours is the body which sings the song
Yours is the mouth with lyrics sweet

May your song be kind to all you meet
May your song rain on every street.

The Music has no body but yours
Yours are the hands, yours are the feet,
Knock down the doors
As the Music pours.

He looked up at the audience from his paper and said, "Mom told me to never forget this. 'Life is a poem written by you and Love'.

So I pass along this wisdom to all of you tonight for these are her words—'be kind to one another.'"

Matt took his seat.

For the encore of the symphony, Lily stood and sang her mother's song, *The Address of Happiness*.

It was as if she had trained all her life for this. Her voice was every bit as unique as her mother's. *Oh,* she thought to herself. *If only she could be here with me now!*

Though we cannot see the heart, we can see the life.

While Lily had just turned fifteen years old, we

saw that she was born for love.

She was born for meaning.

Their mothers would have been proud of their children.

Lily Wilson Eaves would never marry. She would never have children of natural descent.

Her children would be warriors.

For she was brushed with leadership.

Lily would lead the rebellion against the machine people with machine hearts.

In the final days, Lily and her soldiers would fight against the silicon armies.

Through all people, the Music of Love would pour, bringing light to the swords that sped through the darkness.

And the light of their blades would lead the constellations to their destination.

Eventually, Matt would become the author of children's books. He would find the woman that Love had created just for him.

Her name was Emma Towers.

She had a lovely smile and was born to dance. Emma did not suffer fools well and ran her ballet class with authority.

In their marriage, Matt and Emma were fruitful and had many dancers and singers and soccer players. Their children were healthy, aspiring to happy hearts that were forever renewed by the Music.

We are strangers to our own lives, setting out in the dark to look for the adobe of Love which we were meant to know, guided by the Music that wants us to see.

We love against the night, burning like stars against the darkness of bread and circuses.

The happiness in our hearts is there for we dare to dream in light when the world tells us to scream in the darkness.

We are the archers with the bows that spring our children forward.

Life does not go backward, nor does it tarry in yesterday. It is not a circle, but an arrow.

It flies forward with the great express of Love.

All bowmen are caught between heaven and earth, born to discovery, choosing to love and raise their eyes high to a future that is apparent only through the strength of their hope.

For our hope in the future is cosmic, forging human history into eternity.

One day, all those who love in the society of Auld Lang Syne shall meet again.

In the New City of the Burning Heart, there, the veil will drop.

The arc of the seas shall finally know the skies.

Day and night shall end.

The clock tower will crumble.

Time shall fly to the place of no more.

For we were born for meaning.

We were born to love.

There, we shall all be together with all the lovelies ever known who chose mercy and kindness amidst the forget-me-nots and the countless stars.

⁊

Through the celestial envelope, Maddie saw Britney in the twinkling.

It had been so long.

Yet not long at all.

Britney was sitting on Jupiter, her hair tied back from her face.

I have been waiting for you. She sighed and smiled. *...Again.*

Oh, yes.

And Madeline leaned into her with a kiss.

Is this heaven? Madeline asked.

Not quite. This is sort of a commuter stop. But I will take you there. Love said I ought to meet you here so we could walk together.

Really?

Trust me. She smiled.

I always have. She replied.

She took her hand.

What's Love like?

She smiled, growing giddy.

Britney!

What?

What's Love like?

A big crybaby!

And with cheer in her step, Britney ran ahead.

There was the river in front of them. Or was it below them or around them?

It was not clear for reality had changed.

And it was very good.

Matt and Lily will be fine. She said. *You were right to have Hazel raise them.*

I miss them already. She said.

I do too. But they are in good hands.

Do you know how long it has been?

Hours?

Years and years.

Can we watch from here?

Just angels can. But we have so much to learn!

She looked back to Madeline and smiled.

There are no troubles here.

That's what we always believed.

Britney smiled warmly.

In her eyes was the wonder of numerous stars.

She had changed yet her soul remained
the same.

Let's go home.

With that, Britney ran across the trunk of the tree
and onto a tiny branch.

She seemed light for the branch did not bend.

Britney waved and dove into the crystal
blue river.

Madeline looked down.

Britney's soul shone like a white stone in the rain.

With a lovely leap, Madeline followed her,

vanishing for a moment into the living waters of limitless Love.

The river was beautiful and wise. There were the two of them being happy in a new way. There was no man, no woman, no yellow, no black, no white, no old, no young.

Just new. The same but new.

We who were, we are the same no longer.

For there is a river whose streams make glad the city of Love.

Along that river is the tree of heaven.

It is a tree far beyond our imagination….

It's roots lay deep in a holy place which is never-ending.

There we live happily ever after.

For every human idea reaches its limit at the gate of heaven.

But for Love, so we believe.

Dedication

Kay Rochester, my great aunt, recently passed away at the age of 102. She was a feisty, warm-hearted woman who laughed easily, dressed up in costume for every holiday, was an executive at AT&T all her professional life, and loved taking her nephew to every company event to show him off.

Kay was the magic in my world. At her hundredth birthday, she told *The Pittsburgh Gazette* that the secret to her long happy life was due to praying every day and a sherry after Sunday service.

What Kay didn't or couldn't say was that it was also due to her secret love of sixty years.

So with respect, I dedicate this book to Kay Rochester and Dorothy Claybourne, two women of faith and two women in love.

Author's Note

*T**he Address of Happiness**** was inspired by this ancient song. It's lyrics are included for the reader's pleasure and encouragement. I believe it contains lovely language involving the romance between the self and the Divine.

> You have searched me, Lord,
>   and you know me.
> You know when I sit and when I rise;
>   you perceive my thoughts from afar.
> You discern my going out and my lying down;
>   you are familiar with all my ways.
> Before a word is on my tongue
>   you, Lord, know it completely.
> You hem me in behind and before,
>   and you lay your hand upon me.
> Such knowledge is too wonderful for me,
>   too lofty for me to attain.
>
> Where can I go from your Spirit?
>   Where can I flee from your presence?

If I go up to the heavens, you are there;
　　if I make my bed in the depths, you are there.
If I rise on the wings of the dawn,
　　if I settle on the far side of the sea,
　　even there your hand will guide me,
　　your right hand will hold me fast.
If I say, "Surely the darkness will hide me
　　and the light become night around me,"
　　even the darkness will not be dark to you;
　　the night will shine like the day,
　　for darkness is as light to you.

For you created my inmost being;
　　you knit me together in my mother's womb -
I praise you because I am fearfully and wonder
　　fully made; your works are wonderful,
　　I know that full well.
My frame was not hidden from you
　　when I was made in the secret place,
　　when I was woven together in the depths of
　　the earth.
Your eyes saw my unformed body;
　　all the days ordained for me were written in
　　your book before one of them came to be.

How precious to me are your thoughts, God!
    How vast is the sum of them!
Were I to count them,
    they would outnumber the grains of sand -
    when I awake, I am still with you.

Permissions

The lyrics of **Eleanor Rigby** appear by
permission of by Sony/ATV Music Publishing.

The Lyrics from **Somewhere** appear by
permission of the Leonard Bernstein Office, Inc.

The line "We, we who were, we are
the same no longer" originally appeared in
The Saddest Poem by Pablo Neruda.

Acknowledgments

In today's world, no child nor book is raised without many touch points.

I am grateful to Happiness Publishing, especially my editors Ben Wheeler and Molli Jean Kirkpatrick for pouring over the galleys. Paul Lewis created a beautiful layout, elevating the story with his elegant presentation. The creative marketing engine of Scott Mayer, Chris D'Antonio, and Joshua Black was brilliant, connecting this story with our audience.

Thank you, Thom for having the holy fire for this story. You are brave and stout hearted, spearheading *The Address of Happiness* into its completion and into the world. You are my friend.

Emily Clark was always there with helpful support. The ending works because of Monica Bautista's advice. I thank my childhood friend, Elaine McCormick. How could I ever have known the pink-dressed country girl of five would write me such inspiring notes from a New York City skyscraper? I thank Megan Streich for her elegant advice. I also take a bow to my student Steven James Taylor, who has now become my teacher.

I thank my Hollywood friends Ileen Maisel, Marykay Powell, and Anita Busch for their comments and support. Thank you, Doug Collins for your insight, reminding me it was important that Maddie's mother be there for Maddie's time of need. Thank you Don Roos and Dan Bucatinsky.

My wonderful family Sue, Doug, Melinda, Joe, Jim, Ted, Peg, Jane, Harry, Molli, Kelly, and Carey - I would be nothing without your love and kindness. I thank Jack and Bucky Lewis who are the heroes in my life. At the age of 16 and 10, Jack and Bucky traveled to twelve countries serving the world's poor.

I thank all my students, especially Tess Wilson, Billy Stumbo, Jadonna Robinson, and Audrey Kramer for tirelessly scribbling those notes of insight.

A big hug of endless love to the Hollywood pathfinder, Stephen Simon, for writing the generous forward and his gentle heart. His movie, *Somewhere in Time*, is one of my favorite love stories. I also thank Lauren Simon for her love and support.

Finally, I appreciate all the priests, nuns, pastors, and rabbis who have shown their support because they, too, have found the Spirit to be strong in issues that do not conform. Love is radical. Love is fierce, full of fire, yet providing us with restraint and order which is at the center of Love. I lastly thank Henry Wadsworth Longfellow for the inspiration of his heartbreaking poem, "Evangeline, A Tale of Acadie." Evangeline endures to this day as the great poem of destined love.

Through prayer and study, I have come to know this one thing. Within every human heart begs the dance of a sacred romance between two people. May you discover yours.

David Paul Kirkpatrick
April, 2013

facebook.com/theaddressofhappiness

twitter.com/yourhappyplace

pinterest.com/reachhappiness

instagram.com/theaddressofhappiness

www.theaddressofhappiness.com